HOW TO CATCH AN HEIRESS

THE MARRIAGE MAKER BOOK FOUR

TARAH SCOTT

SUE-ELLEN WELFONDER

For all our single readers. We wish you your own Marriage Maker.

CHAPTER 1

CHASTITY HAMILTON, HEIR TO THE ROXBURGH DUKEDOM AND future Duchess of Roxburgh, awoke to the sun streaming through her window and across her bed. Her body warmed through the blanket. The cozy cocoon should have made her burrow deeper beneath the bedding. Instead, something hovered beyond the fuzziness of her sleepy brain. Something was wrong.

Chastity bolted upright. Today was May 30th. Two days before her wedding day. Nae, not just her wedding day--the beginning of her life sentence. How had Sir Stirling managed so quickly to marry her three sisters to three men? She was ashamed to admit she had doubted that three such good men existed. But they did. Within one month's time, Sir Stirling James had married Lucy, her youngest sister, to Baron Delny, the Devil of Delny; Olivia to the privateer—a nice word for pirate—Gordon Frasier; and Jessica, her second youngest sister, to Lieutenant Patrick Chalmers—a navy lieutenant, of all things.

Lucy was the youngest in years, but Chastity had always thought of Jessica as the baby of the family, her kitten, the hoyden who swore she couldn't be tamed and would never marry. Yet Jessica had blossomed into a woman almost overnight, and was thriving as the wife of a strict navy lieutenant. Though, even in the few days they had been married, it was obvious the lieutenant had changed as much as Jessica. Somehow, the two had discovered a middle ground.

Now, as his reward for making three such fine matches, Sir Stirling expected Chastity to honor her agreement and marry him. Determination burned hotly. Sir Stirling had called her a shrew. He had yet to see the shrew. The next two days would open his eyes to the life he would have if he forced her into marriage.

By the sun that poured into her room, Chastity estimated the time as seven-thirty—maybe eight, if she was lucky. She seldom slept even this late. But she'd lain awake worrying about her upcoming nuptials and hadn't fallen asleep until the wee hours of the morning. Sir Stirling was due to arrive at ten to ride with her, and she planned on keeping him waiting. Now, however, it would be her who had to while away the hours until someone came to announce his arrival.

Cook would be baking bread and preparing for the wedding breakfast, which meant Chastity couldn't even get herself a cup of tea. She released a breath. She and Papa were now alone in the house. Never again would Jessica burst into her room to wake her. No longer would she enter the parlor to find Olivia reading a book. Tears unexpectedly stung her eyes. What was wrong with her? She had no reason for sadness. Instead of running after Jessica, and worrying that some fortune hunter would compromise Lucy, and wishing away the sadness in Olivia's eyes, she could delight in knowing that her sisters were happy. Their husbands would care for and protect them for the remainder of their lives, just as Papa had said they would.

But instead of stopping, her tears became sobs, until she

feared a passing maid or even her father might hear. She covered her head with a pillow and pulled the blankets over her body. When force of will failed to control the tears, she finally gave in and let them flow freely.

At last, the tears abated, and shame set in. Was she guilty of her father's charges? Had she sabotaged her sisters' happiness? Meeting the right man had changed Jessica's mind about marriage. Lucy had only just come of age to enter the marriage mart, and Chastity knew she would have married in the next year or two. Then there was Olivia. The two offers she'd received hadn't overly excited her, but was Chastity's contempt for the men the reason Olivia had rejected them?

Olivia's second suitor, Mr. Williams, had been far more respectable than Frasier Gordon, the privateer Olivia married. The problem, in Chastity's estimation, was Mr. Williams' lack of backbone. He was intimidated by Olivia's intellect. Oh, he flattered her, but Chastity knew that once they were married he would have put a stop to her bluestocking ways. Chastity released a breath. Olivia was ridiculously happy with Frasier. Things had worked out just as they should, and Chastity was relieved and happy for her sisters. Olivia and Lucy, in particular, wouldn't have been happy being on the shelf as she was. Her father had been right about that. He had been right about Jessica, as well. Was he right about Sir Stirling?

Chastity shook off the thought. Sir Stirling didn't care for her as her sisters' husbands did them. Now that her sisters were safely—and happily—wed, she could live her life as she pleased, with no man to rule her. All she had to do was get rid of Sir Stirling James.

~

Chastity awoke with a start. Warm sunlight beat down across her bed. She blinked the room into focus, then bolted upright. What time was it? She swung her gaze onto the mantle clock. Ten-fifteen. The fuzziness in her brain persisted, but she knew something wasn't right. Ten-fifteen. Then she remembered. She was supposed to have been ready at ten o'clock to meet Sir Stirling for their morning ride. Why hadn't anyone woken her?

She drew back the covers, jumped to her feet and hurried to the door. Carefully, she eased open the door and peeked into the hallway. Empty. She closed the door and faced the room. What had happened? Her father would never allow her to sleep while Sir Stirling waited for her. The man was late. She pushed from the door and began pacing. How dare he keep her waiting? What sort of gentleman failed to keep his engagements?

She halted. What if something had happened to him? Bah! Nothing had happened. He simply hadn't cared enough to arrive on time. She threw her hands up in exasperation. It was just like him to be late when she'd planned on keeping him waiting. Chastity paused again. She knew only one way to deal with a cad like Sir Stirling.

Half an hour later, Chastity stepped into her mare's saddle and rode out of the stables. A light mist fell. She urged the horse into a gallop down the slope, then turned left when they neared the river. Typically, Chastity loved days like this. To her right, mist rose off the water, giving the morning an ethereal beauty. She often stayed out all day in this kind of weather. Today, however, even the beauty of the rolling hills didn't improve her mood. Seething anger bubbled like a witch's brew in her belly. Sir Stirling hadn't the grace to keep his appointment with her.

Just as you intended to do to him, an inner voice reminded her.

"Because he deserves it," she said aloud.

He probably assumed she would meekly await him in the parlor until he deigned to arrive. Isn't that what wives did? This was the sort of man her father would have her wed. To his credit, Sir Stirling had saved Jessica from Lord John. Goose-flesh raced across her arms with the memory of how loudly Lord John's bones had cracked when Sir Stirling's fist connected with his ribs. Satisfaction swept through her, just as it had when she watched Sir Stirling beat him. The man had deserved every blow Sir Stirling gave him.

Sir Stirling wasn't a bad man, perhaps he was a good man. But he was still a man, and men considered themselves rulers of all they surveyed—and their wives' dictators. Today, Sir Stirling had only proved her point.

How she wished she could see his face when he arrived to find her gone.

A mile from Gledstone Hall, Chastity urged her mare down a gentle slope toward the shore of the loch. An ancient oak grew near the water. She could lay out the plaid she'd brought and sit under the tree to watch the water lap the shore. The book she'd put in her saddlebag would entertain her well into the afternoon, or until she became too chilled to sit outside. She'd even filched a few oatcakes from the kitchen.

She reached the tree, brought the horse to a halt and dismounted. After tying the mare to a nearby sapling, she removed the plaid and book from the saddlebag and spread the blanket on the ground beneath the tree. When she'd settled on the blanket, she set the book on her lap, but turned her attention to the water.

How would she fill her time once she was free of the encumbrances of marriage? Spend days like this, contemplating the world and her place in it? Now that her sisters were married, exactly what was her place in the world? She groaned. Surely, the answer couldn't be that, without her sisters, she had no place. She closed her eyes and released a breath. She would find plenty to do once she dealt with her supposed groom.

The clop of a horse's hooves on the soft ground caused Chastity to yank her attention toward the sound. A rider took shape in the mist. She tensed. Strangers seldom rode across Roxburgh land. She never worried about encountering anyone. She recognized the horse an instant before she realized who the rider must be. Sir Stirling sat erect in the saddle, his hand casually resting on the pommel where he gripped the reins.

How had he found her? Irritation flashed. Her father, of course. He knew this was a favorite spot of hers. She was a fool to think she could find any peace here—or anywhere else, for that matter.

Sir Stirling angled his horse toward her mare, brought it to a halt, dismounted, and tied its reins to the same sapling. He strode to her haven and lowered himself onto the plaid.

She frowned. "It is highly inappropriate for you to come here alone to meet me."

He met her gaze. "No more inappropriate than you riding alone." His words, spoken casually, held a tone of finality.

"Do not think to take me to task for doing something I have done since I was fifteen."

"Your father doesn't care that you ride alone?" he asked.

Her father wasn't aware of her every move. "This is Roxburgh land. It is rare for anyone to happen along, certainly not anyone threatening. We are quite safe here."

He nodded as if he understood, which piqued her ire.

"What are you doing here?" she demanded.

His brows rose in polite surprise. "We had a morning engagement to ride together."

"An engagement that you were late for by forty minutes. I finally decided to set out on my own."

"I believe I arrived at five minutes to eleven. That would make me five minutes early."

Chastity stared. "Early? You were forty minutes late. You were to have been here at ten. You were very precise on that point."

He angled his head. "My apologies. Forgive my tardiness."

The man was patronizing her. "You don't believe you were wrong."

"I have apologized."

She shook her head in disbelief. "An insincere apology. You are placating me."

"I am easy to get along with. Would you rather I insist that you were wrong?"

"You-you—" Chastity let out an unfeminine growl and shoved to her feet. The book on her lap fell to the ground. "You know exactly what you are doing." She whirled and headed for her horse.

She ignored the pad of boots behind her and mounted her mare. Sir Stirling reached his horse as she urged her mare into a trot. Two heartbeats later, the pounding of a horse's hooves approached. She hunkered down and dug her heels into her horse's flanks. The animal broke into a gallop. Wind whipped her hair across her face. The fog had thickened.

"Chastity!" he shouted. "Stop!"

Already, he was ordering her around. She gave her horse its head. If she closed her eyes, she could imagine flying.

He pulled up alongside her. "Don't be a fool," he shouted. "The fog is too thick to ride like this."

Now he was telling her how to ride on the property where she'd grown up. The mare started up another hill. Chastity's stomach swooped. Sir Stirling edged closer, and she realized he intended to seize her reins. A large tree loomed in the mist. She yanked the horse's reins left and brought the animal in a huge circle then stopped. Sir Stirling joined her.

Chastity glimpsed the hard set of his mouth before he said, "Do you feel better?"

She didn't, and she remained silent.

He gave a nod. "Shall we return to Gledstone Hall?"

Chastity clicked her tongue to signal the mare forward, but

Sir Stirling grabbed the reins and said, "At a sedate pace, if you will."

He was right, of course, which only peeved her even more. "As you wish."

He released the reins and she touched the mare with her heels. Sir Stirling waited until she passed and then flanked her.

"Gledstone is this way, my dear." He veered left.

Chastity scanned the area. Fog swirled everywhere, but she'd grown up exploring these hills. She knew how to get home.

"Listen to the water, Chastity," he called. "It is on your left."

She strained her ears, but heard only the beating of her heart.

Sir Stirling stopped and turned his horse toward her. "I spent half my life on water, lass. We want to keep the water to our left in order to reach Gledstone."

When was the last time she'd been lost on Roxburgh land? The holding was not so large that she would easily get lost. But she didn't typically ride in such thick fog. Her father would be furious that she'd gone out in this weather. She could plead ignorance—only mist had drifted off the water when she left Gledstone—but her father wasn't in a charitable mood. She doubted he would care to hear her explanation.

Chastity urged her horse toward Sir Stirling. She reached his side and they rode in silence. She knew she'd lost this battle when a patch of fog cleared enough for her to discern the loch to the left, where Sir Stirling said it was. She was no fool—not completely anyway—and kept her horse to a walk beside his until Gledstone took murky shape ahead. They veered right and, minutes later, rode into the stables. Sir Stirling leapt from his saddle and reached her as she was stepping to the ground. Michael, the groom her father had recently hired, emerged from one of the stalls and hurried toward them.

"I will see you at dinner, Chastity," Sir Stirling said.

"I will tell Cook," she replied stiffly.

He shook his head. "You and your father are coming to Kinlochie Castle tonight."

"What? I have never heard of Kinlochie Castle. Is there a ball there?"

"Kinlochie Castle is my home here in Inverness. The place isn't so grand as to host large balls. Never fear, you may host large parties at my estate in Lossiemouth."

"My father said nothing to me of us dining away from Gledstone."

He flashed a smile. "I spoke with him this morning, before I came looking for you."

Her heart sank. So, her father knew she left before Sir Stirling arrived. What difference did it make? Sir Stirling had been late. She was not obligated to await his convenience.

Tonight, she would be as late for his dinner as he'd been for their ride.

CHAPTER 2

WHEN THE FIRM KNOCK CAME TO CHASTITY'S DOOR AT FOUR-thirty that afternoon, she hurried from the window she stared out of and sat on the couch. She schooled her expression into one of polite disinterest and bid the newcomer—her father, no doubt—enter.

The door opened and the duke stepped inside.

His eyes flicked from the dress laid out on the bed to her. "Tell me, Chastity, what have I done last month that would convince you that I am incapable of carrying out every threat I have made?"

She shrugged. "Nothing."

"Yet you sit there and aren't dressed for dinner."

"You can do nothing more to me than what you have planned," she said with an airy wave of her hand.

"Whether you marry today or the day after tomorrow matters not?" he asked.

She lifted her shoulders in another careless shrug.

A gleam entered his eyes. "Then perhaps the choice of groom might matter."

Chastity frowned. "What do you mean?"

"All actions have consequences, Chastity. You believe I will let your behavior go unchecked?" Dread slithered along the inside of her stomach. "The special license I have obtained does not specify the groom."

She forced calm. "The groom is Sir Stirling James. He has worked hard for the honor of carrying on your title. He is not about to give that up."

Determination glinted in his eyes. "I am the Duke of Roxburgh. Sir Stirling cannot stop me if I decide to marry you to another man."

Her heartbeat accelerated. "And what if Sir Stirling should decide he doesn't want me, what then? Will you force me to marry Lord Hathaway?"

Fury flashed in his eyes. "Aye."

An answering anger swept through her. "Your three younger daughters have married. If I do not, the title will fall to Olivia and her husband upon my death. You have assured that the title will not die. They are happy. Why must you insist I marry?"

He drew back his shoulders. "My word still means something—even if yours does not. It was you who proposed this arrangement. It is your own fault that you didn't believe I could find someone to take up your challenge. I did. Therefore, Sir Stirling deserves his reward."

"Yet you continue to threaten me with marriage to Lord Hathaway—at the risk of breaking your own word to Sir Stirling."

"Aye, because you continue to defy me at every turn. Mark my words, if you try to thwart Sir Stirling, I will marry you to Hathaway."

"Mark *my* words, Father. If you marry me to Lord Hathaway, I will guarantee that you have no grandchild from our union."

His gaze sharpened. "Then his bastard will take my title."

She gasped. "You would rob Olivia of the title just to spite me?"

"Nae." He shook his head. "It is you who would do that. I know exactly what you plan. You intend to avail yourself of all the advantages of my title until the day you die. Then you will leave the title to Olivia. It is unfair that you get the advantages and shoulder none of the responsibility."

"None of the responsibility?" she cried. "I have been responsible for your three daughters the last eight years."

He nodded. "Aye, and that was wrong. I should have remarried. But after your mother died I—" He broke off.

Chastity stared. She knew her parents' marriage had been a love match, but she hadn't considered that her father might have felt her loss as keenly as they had.

"You still miss her," Chastity whispered. "You never said anything."

He shrugged. "What should I have said? A father doesn't burden his daughters with the loss of his wife when they have lost their mother. I was wrong not to remarry." A strange look entered his eyes. "All of you girls—you in particular—would have been better off with the guiding hand of a mother."

She fought tears. "We did well."

He lifted a brow. "Indeed? You hate marriage and I have no idea why."

"It isn't that I hate marriage," she said. "I simply do not wish to be governed by another man."

His gaze softened. "Has life been so bad living under my protection?"

In truth, she had generally done as she pleased. But that she was not going to admit.

He nodded slowly. "I believe I see. Under my protection, you have lived as you wished. With a husband, however, you fear that freedom will be lost. You are right. No husband would allow his wife to do exactly as she likes in all things. I was wrong to allow you so much freedom."

"See!" she exclaimed. "That is exactly the point. Men live as free as birds. Women, however, have no power to make a man do anything—including treating them properly."

"You're wrong." A shadow flickered across his face. "Women wield great power. Your mother owned me body and soul."

"So you say." Chastity snorted. "Mama had to get your permission to spend your money. The property she owned became yours."

"Nae," he cut in. "Her property remained hers. Even now, Lenydale is in your name."

"What? But the law—"

"The law does not compel me to take possession of her property."

"Perhaps not, but it allows you to take it."

"If I please. But I didn't. Contrary to what you believe, Chastity, some men do believe women are intelligent."

"Being intelligent is well enough. But we must hide our intelligence—as you counseled Olivia to do."

"You would have sent Olivia to a university filled with men, teachers, and students, who believed she shouldn't be there? Do you believe she would have returned home unscathed?"

Chastity started. "What do you mean?"

"You know exactly what I mean."

"Surely you don't believe anyone would've harmed her?"

He gave her a disgusted look. "I thought you had more sense. Most men—and women—are not so enlightened as to accept that women are equal to men. She would have returned home with her dignity—and her virtue—ripped from her. Now get dressed for dinner."

"I will relinquish the title to Olivia."

"You will dress for dinner."

"What does it matter who carries on the title?" she asked.

He shook his head. "By God, you would have me leave you in spinsterhood to rely upon the goodwill of your sisters and their husbands?"

"A thousand pounds a year will support me."

"Not very well."

"Well enough," she insisted. "If Sir Stirling truly does not want me, then release me from my responsibility."

He studied her. "You would rather give up your place in the family than marry?"

She scowled. "I am not giving up my place. I will still be the eldest sister of the clan."

He hesitated and she pressed the advantage. "You would be assured of the proper training for Olivia's son as the next duke. I wouldn't be reaping the rewards without the penalty."

"You cannot avoid Sir Stirling. You cannot run away. You cannot say no if he says yes. No matter what, if he gets ye to the altar, then you must produce an heir." She started to reply, but he added, "Defy me in this in any way, and I swear on your mother's grave that I will divorce you from Sir Stirling then marry you to a young vicar who believes it's God's will that he govern his wife with an iron fist."

"Done," she said.

What had she to lose?

❧

STIRLING SIPPED HIS WINE, THEN SET THE GLASS ON THE TABLE beside his dinner plate and politely listened as Chastity explained to his dinner guests, Mr. Dorring and Lord Allensby, how the duke's young groom had broken their new gelding. The duke must have had a talk with his daughter. She was being far too accommodating, and that worried him. He much preferred a frontal assault like the one this morning. At least then he knew what she was up to. This...this was dangerous. They'd been late to dinner, which was exactly what he'd expected after he kept her waiting nearly an hour this morning. But she'd been a different woman than the one he'd left at the stables this morning. He would have to talk with the duke and find out what had happened, then ask him to kindly stay out of the way.

Her gaze caught on his face and she flashed a sweet smile. Yes, this troubled him far more than her obstinacy. There wasn't a chance in heaven or hell that her father had convinced her to go meekly to the altar. What was the minx planning? Maybe she planned on boring him to death? He hid a smile. Nae, not that one. She wasn't capable of being boring for more than an evening, and that, he suspected, was part of a larger plan.

They finished dinner and the six men adjourned to the drawing room with the promise that they would meet the ladies in the parlor once they'd had their cigars and brandy. Stirling couldn't remain focused on the conversation. It bothered him not knowing what Chastity was thinking. Until now, she had been an open book and he'd easily kept one step ahead of her. If she drew from the feminine arsenal, the more common tactic of backhanded manipulation, he might be in trouble.

"Where is your mind, Stirling?" the Earl of Allensby broke into his thoughts. "Certainly, not with that pretty girl you are to marry?"

Stirling couldn't help a laugh. He hadn't been this distracted by a woman in ten years, maybe never, in fact. "Can you blame me?"

Allensby grinned. "If a man must be shackled to a woman, she isn't a bad choice."

Stirling was aware of the duke's attention, so lifted his glass of brandy and answered honestly, "I couldn't agree more."

They finished their cigars and all took their brandies to the parlor where, to Stirling's relief, Chastity was engaged in a game of cards with the three ladies. She didn't look his way, but he felt certain she was aware of his presence the minute he entered the room. Or perhaps that was just wishful thinking.

Chastity suggested the men join them for cards and she didn't shoot daggers at him with her eyes when he pulled a chair up alongside hers and sat down. As the evening wore on, Chastity did seem at ease. Stirling had just begun to relax a bit himself—the brandy didn't hurt on that score—then he noticed Linda Dorring staring at him. She didn't yank her eyes away as he expected and he stiffened when a slippered foot traced a line up his calf.

What the bloody hell? Stirling hadn't known Dorring long, and had no idea if he and his wife had an *arrangement*, but he didn't dally with married women even if their husbands looked the other way. And he wasn't pleased with her overt behavior. If Chastity noticed, it could be the justification she needed to end their engagement. And there it was, he realized. Linda Dorring's sudden interest in him was too convenient. Chastity had to have sanctioned her advances. Stirling shot Linda a thin-lipped look, then shifted his legs beyond reach of her foot.

She thrust out her lip in a very pretty pout that disgusted Stirling. He couldn't believe Dorring didn't notice his wife's behavior. But then, maybe he did and ignored it. He might be too accustomed to this sort of conduct.

They finished the game and Stirling rose. "Who would like more brandy?"

The men all agreed more brandy was a good idea. To Stirling's relief, the women rose. Chastity crossed to the open balcony and stood on the threshold. He filled glasses with brandy and handed one to each man. When he grabbed his glass from the sideboard, he saw that Chastity had disappeared. She must have gone out onto the balcony.

Fortunately, everyone was engaged in conversation. He slipped out and found her leaning her elbows against the railing, staring out across the darkened hills. She looked over her shoulder as he approached and he glimpsed the roll of her eyes before she turned away. He repressed a smile. This, he understood.

He stopped beside her and sipped his brandy. "It's a lovely night."

"It is."

"Castle Kinlochie may lack a view of the River Ness, but the castle is respectable. I hope you will be happy here."

She visibly stiffened. "As the Duchess of Roxburgh, I will one day live at Gledstone Hall."

"Let us pray that day does not come for some time."

She straightened and faced him. "Are you implying that I am waiting for my father to die so that I can claim the title?"

"Not at all. Like you, I am wishing your father many more years of health and happiness."

"The longer he lives, the longer you must wait to become duke."

"True." Stirling sipped his brandy.

"How long are you willing to wait for your reward?" she asked.

"Approximately thirty-six hours."

She blinked, then narrowed her eyes. "I am not fooled by your sweet words."

He kept his gaze locked with hers. Aye, he was certain Chastity was behind Linda Dorring's advances. Perhaps her pique was heightened because that plot had failed.

"There is nothing to be fooled by, my lady. What have I to gain by false flattery?"

Her mouth thinned. "My goodwill."

He chuckled. "Honest flattery will accomplish that much quicker."

She scowled. "Does nothing make you angry? Wait," she added before he could reply, "my leaving without you this morning made you angry."

He shook his head. "Nae. Your foolhardy actions concerned me."

"Foolhardy?" She snorted. "This entire plot you have hatched is foolhardy."

"Forgive me for disagreeing, but your sisters are happily married. That is not foolhardy."

To his surprise, she didn't respond with a quick retort. Instead, she studied him for a long moment. "I find it interesting you knew just the right three men for my sisters."

He flashed a smile. "Some would call that fate."

"Some might call it strangely fortunate."

"I am a very fortunate man." He took a step closer. "Especially now that I am to marry you."

She blinked and seemed at a loss for words. The reaction lasted but an instant before her eyes narrowed again. "As I said, your flattery is wasted."

He stepped even closer. "What will do me good?"

She gave a small gasp of surprise. The sound sent a message directly to his cock and it took every ounce of will he had not to crush her to him. Not quite yet could he let her know the depth of his desire. In many ways, she wasn't the typical female. He detected no true deceit in her, but she was still a woman, and could be cagey if the need arose. He couldn't chance her anticipating his moves.

She stared up at him, brown eyes wide, like a deer caught unawares. When he finally kissed her, he wanted her cognizant of its meaning.

Like a frightened deer, she retreated a step, and he didn't attempt to stop her when she hurried back inside. Stirling stared at the doorway where she'd disappeared. Roxburgh had told him she eloped four years ago. The duke made it clear that there was no guarantee that her virtue remained intact. Chastity didn't act like a woman who'd once had a lover. Was it possible she was still a virgin and feared the marriage bed?

He gave a low laugh. It was far more possible she was simply afraid of the way he made her feel.

CHAPTER 3

FOR THE SECOND NIGHT IN A ROW, CHASTITY LAY AWAKE MOST OF the night. She told herself that any woman being forced into marriage wouldn't be able to sleep. But her mind kept returning to the moment when Sir Stirling had stepped so close that she could smell the sweet brandy on his breath. *"What would do me some good?"* he'd murmured in a husky voice that sent a shiver down her arms.

The man had been flirting with her. Nae, this was more than flirting. This was seduction. He was very, very dangerous.

She prayed the plan she had set in motion would put an end to their betrothal.

In the morning, when the wake-up knock came to her door, Chastity was already sitting at the small secretary in her room. She spent the day in her room, uninterrupted by anyone, her father included. Thankfully Sir Stirling didn't make an appearance at Gledstone Hall until nine p.m., when he arrived to pick up her and her father for the ball at the Marquess of Byrne's home. This time, Chastity was ready when Sir Stirling arrived. When the evening's events came to light, her father would not be able to accuse her of causing problems.

Sir Stirling made polite conversation and complimented her on how beautiful she looked. "We shan't stay out too late, my lady," he said. "I know how you love to rise early."

He knew nothing of the sort, but she smiled and thanked him.

They arrived at the marquess' home, and when they entered the ballroom, Chastity was a bundle of nerves. Guilt began to pick at her, but she battled the feeling with the understanding that she would make Sir Stirling a terrible wife. She was doing them both a favor by making sure they didn't marry.

Of course, if Sir Stirling proved to be unique among his sex, her plan would fail and she would accept her fate. But the man who had stared down at her with such intense desire was not a man to turn away a beautiful woman. The duke would not countenance his eldest daughter, the future Duchess of Roxburgh, marrying a man who made love to another woman the night before he was to wed his daughter.

Chastity thought of her sisters' three husbands. She didn't know the men well, but they did appear to be in love with their wives. If Sir Stirling had expressed any kind of real affection for her, she might have considered a different path. But what was she losing by breaking off an engagement to a man who only wanted her father's title?

Lady Byers rushed to greet them. "Your Grace." She dropped into a deep curtsy.

He grasped her hand and urged her upright. "Thank you for having us here tonight."

"It is my pleasure." She turned to Chastity. "Lady Chastity, you are looking fine."

Chastity angled her head. "As always, you are beautiful, Lady Byers."

The lady gave her attention to Sir Stirling and extended her hand. "A pleasure, as always, sir."

He grasped her gloved hand and dutifully bent over it. He

was the modicum of proper manners, but Chastity had the strange feeling that there was a history between them.

He straightened and released her hand.

She again faced the Duke. "If you would like to come with me, Your Grace, I'm sure my husband will be pleased to see you."

He looked at Sir Stirling, who said, "As you will, Your Grace. Chastity and I will dance." His eyes swung onto her. "If she will do me the honor."

Chastity angled her head in agreement, and her father left with Lady Byers. Sir Stirling led her toward the dance floor. As she feared, they were immediately set upon.

"Lady Chastity."

Chastity looked left and saw the young Miss Doncaster approaching. Chastity groaned at sight of the three women who hurried to keep up with her. Sir Stirling turned toward the young women, and Chastity glimpsed the laughter that tugged at his mouth.

Miss Doncaster reached them first and said, "How wonderful to see you, my lady. We were certain you wouldn't be here, what with your wedding tomorrow." She cast a knowing glance at her friends. The nearest, Lady Madeleine, a girl of seventeen, clearly should have remained home with her school chums. She looked at Sir Stirling with such adoration that Chastity had to force back an eye roll. Sir Stirling looked at Chastity, brows raised, clearly half amused and half urging her to properly introduce him to the young ladies.

Chastity reminded herself of her goal tonight, and smiled sweetly. "Sir Stirling, may I introduce Miss Doncaster, Lady Madeleine--" Chastity nodded at the adoring blonde. "Lady Henrietta, and Lady Sanders."

The girls each blushed when Sir Stirling bent over their hands, and Chastity wondered if she'd ever been that dewy-eyed. Nae, she didn't think so. Like Jessica, Chastity left the womb just as she was today: practical, levelheaded, and unromantic. Even when she eloped with Everston, she hadn't had stars in her eyes as these girls did.

True, she'd misjudged him—or, at least, had misjudged her situation. His character wasn't a bad one. He had—she still believed—loved her, and she had loved him. Or so she thought. Seeing her sisters so happy made her wonder if she understood love at all, or if she'd experienced it as she thought she had. Her father may not have been as wrong as she thought to have forbidden the marriage. She shook off her thoughts and realized Miss Doncaster was speaking.

"How amazing that you and your sisters are marrying in so short a period of time. We had no idea any of you were engaged."

"So unusual," Lady Henrietta said. "Will you marry by special license, as your sisters did?"

"Of course they will," Miss Doncaster said. "There has been only the one announcement in the papers for their engagement."

Chastity's mind snapped to attention. Was that censure she heard in the girl's voice? Yes, but there was more. The girl was jealous. The young ladies very obviously had stopped Chastity and Sir Stirling in order to obtain an introduction to a handsome, wealthy man. But there was more in Miss Doncaster's comments.

Chastity looked down her nose at the girl. "Miss Doncaster, I feel certain that you do not mean to imply that there was a 'need' for my sisters and I to marry?"

The girl's eyes widened. The other young ladies looked at her in confusion.

"Need?" Lady Madeleine said, then her eyes widened as well. "Oh, my, no, Lady Chastity. We did not mean to imply that at all. We think it's romantic."

"I was not addressing you, Lady Madeleine," Chastity said in frosty tones.

Miss Doncaster blanched. "Oh no, my lady, I did not mean to imply that at all. Please forgive the misunderstanding."

"I advise you not to give anyone else that impression, even by mistake," she said. "The duke would not be pleased."

Miss Doncaster's eyes widened even more. "Nae, my lady, of course not." She glanced at her friends. "Come, ladies, I cannot be long away from my mother." She curtsied to Chastity. "It was a pleasure to see you, my lady." She whirled and hurried away, her friends in tow.

"Remind me never to make you angry."

Chastity jerked her gaze onto Sir Stirling. Unbridled male delight danced in his eyes. "You will make a brilliant duchess."

Chastity scowled. "That was your handiwork."

His brow shot up. "Mine? How so?"

"If you hadn't rushed my sisters to the altar, no one would suspect impropriety."

"Forgive me, but I believe it was you who insisted on the month deadline."

"Only because I didn't believe anyone could accomplish such a thing," she muttered.

His expression turned downright wicked. "Now you know."

Chastity started. Aye, the man was dangerous.

CHAPTER 4

STIRLING SCANNED THE BALLROOM FOR CHASTITY. HE WAS positive she was up to something. She was being too nice. He suspected that even under the best of circumstances, she wasn't overly 'nice' to anyone. The woman was a born duchess. The set-down she'd given Miss Doncaster had been brilliant. Chastity had looked down her nose at the girl like a true aristocrat. And the young lady had deserved everything Chastity had dished out.

Chastity wasn't made to be amenable, and yet she was being far too amenable.

He caught sight of her on the left side of the ballroom, hurrying toward a hallway. She glanced back and he tensed. That look had been odd. She acted as if she didn't want anyone to see her.

He started across the ballroom, dodging guests and brushing off greetings. He reached the hallway and quickened pace. Light footsteps echoed up ahead. He turned a corner and heard the click of a door shutting, up ahead on the left. What the devil was she up to? Surely, she wouldn't go so far as to compromise herself in order to get him to break their betrothal? Stirling quickened pace. Whoever the man was, Stirling would kill him.

He reached the room and burst inside. A low fire burned in the study's hearth. Something rustled on the divan that faced the fire. Stirling crossed the room, skirted two chairs and rounded the couch. He halted at sight of the naked woman sprawled on the cushions.

Linda Dorring stared up at him. "I thought you would never get here," she purred.

Confusion quickly gave way to understanding. Chastity didn't intend to compromise herself. She intended to compromise him. He wanted to laugh. The lass had no understanding of the ways of men. She counted on her father protecting her from a rake who would bed a woman on the eve of his marriage. Stirling wouldn't do something so despicable, and he would wager the duke knew that. His Grace was sure to see through the plot and marry her to Hathaway, as he'd threatened. That, Stirling could not allow.

He turned and headed for the door. Two paces from the door, he stopped when the duke stepped into the threshold. Stirling silently cursed. No matter, he would turn things around.

"Your Grace," he said. "I am in a bit of a hurry."

The duke's gaze shifted past him. Linda Dorring gasped, and a small thud told Stirling she'd fallen off the couch. The duke's eyes narrowed and swung back to Stirling's.

"I only just arrived and, as you can see, I'm fully dressed with not a hair out of place—and I nearly collided with you on my way out the door," Stirling said.

The duke's expression hardened. "Then what is this about?"

"Your daughter's handiwork, I suspect."

The older man blinked, then his expression turned thunderous. "This goes too far. I release you of all obligation—in fact, I would not wish my daughter off on a man of your caliber. I will marry her to Hathaway first thing tomorrow."

Behind Stirling, something dragged across the floor, but he ignored the sound, and said, "We have an agreement, Your Grace, and I intend to hold you to it."

Surprise shown on the duke's face. "You cannot want her after this."

Stirling chuckled. "As strange as it is, I want her more."

The duke frowned. "I wonder if Chastity is correct. Are you mad?"

"In all likelihood, I am. What man who wants to marry isn't just a little bit mad?"

The older man's expression turned speculative. "Are you saying it is not the title you want, but my daughter?"

Stirling nodded in the direction of the hallway. "Perhaps we should speak outside."

The duke backed up two paces and Stirling followed, pulling the door closed behind him. He took several steps away from the door. The duke followed.

Stirling slowed, took a few more steps, then stopped and faced the duke. "In truth, sir, I have no need for the title."

"I'll be damned," the duke murmured. "I love my daughter, but I must ask, why?"

Stirling shrugged. "She is magnificent."

The duke's brow furrowed, then his expression cleared. "She is more like her mother than I care to admit."

"I imagine, then, she was a rather magnificent woman, as well," Stirling said.

A soft light entered the older man's eyes. "More than I can convey."

"Then you understand how I feel."

The duke gave a slow nod. "When I shared Chastity's ridiculous scheme to marry off her sisters, you were quick to accept the challenge. I believed you saw the opportunity to elevate your station in life. It never occurred to me you had any other interest."

"You couldn't know. Now, if you'll excuse me, I feel I must deal with my future bride."

To Stirling's surprise, the duke laughed. "Do what you think best. Take my advice, lad, and remember that the Roxburgh women are as intelligent as they are beautiful."

Stirling grinned. "I am counting on that very thing, sir." He started to turn away, then stopped. "Would you consider helping me teach your daughter a lesson?"

His brows rose. "What sort of lesson?"

"Am I right in assuming that someone sent you to this room?"

The duke reached into his pocket and pulled out a small sliver of paper. He unfolded it and handed it to Stirling. The note read 'Please meet me in the study. Second door on the left down the hallway.'

Stirling nodded. "Lady Chastity believed you would catch me in the throes of an illicit encounter. I imagine she believed you would call off our engagement, and pack her off home, and that would be the end of that. It never occurred to her that had you caught me with another woman, you might feel the need to defend her honor."

A slow smile spread across the duke's face. "In the future, she might think twice about dabbling in such an idiotic plan if she better understood the consequences. She will spend a sleepless night tonight, wondering which one of us will kill the other in defense of her honor."

"It is a hard lesson," Stirling said.

"One she dearly needs to learn," he replied.

"I will enter the ballroom first and do my best to make sure she sees me leave. If you find her immediately and tell her you're leaving, she will assume you caught me with Mrs. Dorring."

The duke nodded. "She will, of course, try to get me to tell her what happened."

"Exactly. Tomorrow, you can inform her that you spoke with me, and came to understand that I wasn't engaged in a rendezvous with the woman, but that I had tried to extricate myself from the situation. You do understand, I would not have her think that I would do that to her?"

The duke nodded. "Of course. You go along. I will follow in a few minutes."

A moment later, Stirling turned the bend in the hallway and slowed at the sound of voices inside the room to his left. Was that Chastity's voice? He crept to the door and strained to hear the voices beyond the thick wood. He discerned the muffled sound of the man's voice, but couldn't discern the words. The woman cried out.

Stirling threw open the door. Mr. Dorring held Chastity pinned against the sideboard located beside a small hearth. Chastity seized the clock from the mantle and bashed the side of his head.

He cried out as Stirling lunged forward. Chastity's gaze snapped onto him, eyes wide. Stirling seized Dorring's arm, and threw an upper cut to his jaw. Dorring flew backwards and crashed into a small table, then he hit the floor, and rolled to his feet as Stirling leapt toward him. Dorring drove a fist into Stirling's gut. Stirling was vaguely aware of Chastity's scream as he drove Dorring backward. They collided with another table and lamp.

Dorring threw an arm around Stirling's throat. Stirling hauled Dorring over his shoulder. The man hit the carpet on his back, then pushed to his knees. Chastity stepped into view and before Stirling could speak she whacked him across the side of the face with a large book. The man wavered. Stirling started toward him, then large hands seized his shoulders and yanked him backwards. He ripped free and whirled, fist raised.

"Stop!" Chastity shouted.

Stirling registered the duke's face and froze. He heaved in heavy breaths.

"What happened?" the duke demanded.

Stirling swung on Chastity. "Mr. Dorring assaulted Chastity."

The duke's eyes jerked onto her. "Is this true?"

She nodded.

"What the blazes were you doing alone with him?"

She opened her mouth to reply, then looked helplessly at Stirling. Dorring moaned and opened his eyes. Stirling lunged for him. The duke seized his arm and yanked him back.

"He is unconscious. You will hang for killing a defenseless man."

"I don't give a damn," Stirling snapped.

The man sat up and blinked. "She came with me of her own accord, you bastard," he snapped at Stirling.

"You asked to speak with me, sir," she said. "I had no intention of engaging in an illicit encounter with you."

He touched his head and grimaced. "A lady doesn't agree to meet a man alone unless she--"

Stirling yanked free of the two and reached Dorring in two bounds. He drove his fist into the man's jaw. They hit the floor and rolled. Again, the duke pulled Stirling off Dorring.

"Enough," the duke shouted.

"Aye," Stirling growled. "Tomorrow morning, Dorring. The clearing near Kinlochie Castle."

"What?" Dorring blinked. "You can't be serious. No one duels anymore."

Stirling gave a harsh laugh. "Your ignorance only demonstrates your cowardice. Dueling is very much alive among men of honor."

"Among fools, perhaps." Dorring pushed to his feet.

Stirling gave him a cold smile. "Then I must be the greatest of fools. Tomorrow morning at dawn."

Chastity gasped.

"I don't duel," Dorring said. "It is illegal."

"Be there, or I will pull you out of bed and drag you there."

Dorring looked at the duke. "Reason with him, Your Grace."

The duke's expression hardened. "Chastity is my daughter. If James doesn't kill you, I will."

"Papa," Chastity cried.

"Silence," he ordered.

Dorring looked from the duke to Chastity, then stormed from the room.

Chastity rushed to her father's side. "Papa, Mr. Dorring is right. Dueling is illegal—not to mention dangerous. Someone could get killed."

He regarded her. "You should have thought of that before you came to this room alone with him. What in God's name possessed you? You know better."

She shook her head. "He said he needed to speak with me."

"Speak with you? What could he possibly have to speak with you about?" His gaze bored into her and Stirling felt sorry for her.

"Your Grace, it was an innocent mistake," Stirling said.

"Was it?" He still glared at her.

"I can deal with Dorring," Stirling said. "There is no need to worry the lass."

"I ask you again, Chastity," the duke's gaze locked on her face, "what could Dorring possibly have to speak with you about?"

"Sir," Stirling began, but she cut him off.

"He is right. I shouldn't have been here alone with Mr. Dorring. I am to blame."

"You meant no harm," Stirling said.

"Aye, but I did. I intended to tarnish your reputation."

He nodded. "I know."

"What?" She looked from him to her father, then collapsed onto the chair beside her. "Oh dear, that's why you're together. I have made a mess of everything."

Her father opened his mouth to reply, but Stirling said, "Not so big a mess."

Her father gave him a nod, and Chastity realized Sir Stirling had saved her from a well-deserved set-down. An unexpected desire to cry surfaced and she feared she would further embarrass herself.

Chastity took a breath and rose. "No harm was done. There is no need to endanger yourself by meeting Mr. Dorring tomorrow at dawn."

Sir Stirling smiled gently. "You may not understand, Lady Chastity, but there is every need to meet him tomorrow."

"Please do not give me the drivel that your manly honor must be preserved."

His expression further softened. "Nae, my lady, it is your honor that must be upheld."

CHAPTER 5

Chastity had been certain she couldn't make matters any worse, but now, riding in a darkened carriage at 3 a.m., she wasn't so sure. Her father's stablemaster, John, accompanied her. The man had served them fifteen years, and was an honest and good man.

They passed a parked carriage, then, a moment later, the carriage came to a halt.

The vehicle shifted and, in the next instant, John opened the door. Chastity gave her hand to him and descended from the coach, her eyes on the Dorring's mansion. The place was completely dark. In the moonless night, some small light should indicate that at least a small fire burned in some of the rooms.

Chastity frowned. Surely Mr. Dorring couldn't be sleeping the hour before he was to meet Sir Stirling for a duel? Had he fled? She mouthed a quick prayer that their problems would be solved so easily—and promised absolute obedience from now on, if God granted such salvation.

"Please wait," Chastity told the driver. "Come along, John." She started up the walkway.

They reached the door and she lifted the heavy knocker and knocked three times. Bootfalls on the walkway behind them drew her attention. She turned as a man hurried toward them. Chastity squinted in the darkness to discern the approaching stranger's identity. Something familiar niggled. He neared them and John stepped in front of her.

"For God's sake, Chastity, what are you doing here?"

"Sir Stirling?" She slipped past John.

He climbed the first stair, but John stepped toward him.

"Never mind, John." Chastity stopped as Sir Stirling climbed the next two steps. He grasped her arm and started down the stairs. "What are you doing?" she demanded.

"Taking you home, where you belong."

She tried to yank free, but his grip tightened. "I have no intention of going home until you agree to forget this ridiculous duel."

He ignored her and kept walking.

Chastity looked over her shoulder. "John, quickly come here."

"By God, Chastity, if you make me fight your manservant, I will take you over my knee and paddle your pretty behind."

Chastity yanked her gaze onto him. "You wouldn't dare."

He gave a mirthless laugh." Not only would I dare, I would do so with relish. Now call off your bulldog."

"He is not my bulldog. He is my protector. And I need protecting."

Sir Stirling barked a laugh. "It is I who need protection from you." Sir Stirling whirled. "Stay right there, lad," he said to John, who halted two paces away. "As you know, I am the lady's fiancé. Now, I am taking her home."

"You are taking me home?" Chastity asked.

He cast her a look she couldn't discern in the dim light. "You would like that. Nae, your protector will escort you home.

Come along, protector, you will return home with Lady Chastity."

"Do not listen to him, John," she said. "You are to stay here with me."

"Well, what's it to be, John?" Sir Stirling asked.

"I must do as Lady Chastity commands," John replied.

"Then I shall have to fight you. I promise to go easy on you because I understand you are doing only what your mistress commands you to do."

"You're mad," Chastity said. "First you challenge Mr. Dorring a duel, then you would fight John. Is this how you live your life, sir? For I must tell you, you are a barbarian."

"Forgive me, my lady, but I must point out that both these instances are your doing."

She started to reply, then stopped. He was right. "I beg you, do not duel with Mr. Dorring." Chastity's thought skidded to a halt. Why was she arguing? The house was dark. It was clear no one was home. The coward had fled. Still, if she was wrong, she would never forgive herself if anything happened to Sir Stirling. A thought occurred to her.

"I will leave, if you leave."

"Will you now?"

Something in his tone gave her pause.

"Do not move from the spot." Without waiting for a reply, he released her and strode in the direction of the other coach parked down the street. He reached the other coach, opened the door and said something in low tones, then returned to where she stood. He grasped her arm and started forward.

"What are you doing?"

"Taking you home."

"This isn't at all what I had in mind."

"Then I suggest that the next time you be more precise."

They reached the coach and Sir Stirling said to the driver as he opened the door, "Sir, when this door closes, you are to return to the lady's home with all speed. I will pay you double your fare." He didn't wait for an answer, but swung her into his arms and stepped inside the carriage.

"Have you lost your mind?" she cried as he dropped onto the seat.

She was immediately aware of the hard thighs beneath her bottom and a dizzying current swept through her. He crushed her to his chest and held her with one arm while he pulled the door shut with the other, which left them in murky darkness. The coach lurched into motion.

"Release me," she demanded. To her surprise, he lifted her from his lap and tossed her onto the opposite cushion. She bounced and listed to the left but caught herself with her hand and righted herself. "I will not tolerate this sort of behavior in a husband," she snapped.

"And I should tolerate this sort of behavior in a wife?"

She wanted to reply but, for the first time in her life, words failed her. "Forget the duel, Sir Stirling. It is likely he has fled. The house is dark. No one was home."

"Then you have nothing to fear."

She fell silent for a long moment, then said, "I cannot allow you to be killed on my account."

He didn't reply. She thought perhaps he didn't intend to. Then he said, "Wouldn't that solve your problems?"

She snorted. "Indeed, it would. But I am not that heartless."

They both fell silent again for several heartbeats.

"Why would you defend my honor after..." She couldn't finish the sentence.

"A man always defends his fiancée's honor."

"Do you really want to be a duke so badly that you would marry a woman who tried to discredit you?"

He frowned. "Discredit me? You know very little about men if you think something as mundane as bedding a woman can discredit him."

She stiffened. "I see."

"You don't see, at all. At worst, had your plan worked, your father would have called off our engagement. You weren't really trying to hurt me. You have simply set your mind against our marriage."

She experienced an irrational desire to stick her tongue out at him. "Are you always so unreasonably reasonable?"

He laughed the same laugh she'd grown accustomed to, and she tried to ignore the warmth that spread through her. "It's a curse," he said.

"Are you saying that you didn't take advantage of the situation with Mrs. Dorring?" she asked.

"I believe all of ten minutes passed between the time I found her and the time I discovered you with Dorring. Perhaps we have hit upon the reason you don't want to marry me."

She frowned. "What do you mean?"

"If you think I spend no more than ten minutes in a lady's company before we part ways, then I can see why you would find me an undesirable husband."

"I don't know what you mean." Her face flushed. She did know what he meant.

"Perhaps I have made a mistake in not showing you one of the biggest advantages in being my wife."

"What—"

He shifted and she started when he grasped her waist and she once again found herself sitting across his hard thighs.

"Sir Stirling—"

He pulled her against his chest. "Am I really such an ogre?" he asked.

His warm breath bathed her cheek. Her heart jumped to a gallop.

"Have I no redeeming qualities?" he murmured.

Her mind muddled. She hadn't been this close to a man since she'd eloped with Lord Everston. Sir Stirling shifted and she realized he intended to kiss her. Chastity froze when his lips brushed hers. He gently grasped her neck and stroked her ear with his thumb. A shiver slid down the back of her neck and across her shoulders when his mouth fully covered hers.

Dangerous, her mind whispered.

Chastity fisted his lapel as his mouth moved on hers. She noted the bulge that pressed against her hip. Surely, lust hadn't affected him so quickly? He broke the kiss and pressed his lips to her ear. She shivered. His mouth closed around her lobe and he nibbled. The carriage jostled and she bumped his hard length. He drew in a sharp breath. He bit down a little harder on her ear.

Lord, she'd never felt anything so decadent. Lord Everston was a skilled lover—or so she'd thought—but he hadn't made her tremble by merely nibbling on her ear. Nibbling on her ear? The idea seemed somehow indecent. And why not? The way he made her feel was indecent. Her nipples hardened and pressed against the fabric of her corset. His mouth slid down her neck to her shoulder. He tugged one sleeve down and she started when his mouth made contact with the rise of her breast.

This was improper and she should put a stop to it. But her mind remained frozen as his tongue slipped below the edge of her corset and flicked her nipple. His breath tickled the sensitive flesh, causing shivers to race down her abdomen straight to the juncture between her legs. The hand cupping her neck slid around her neck and started downward. Her heart beat faster as his fingers molded to her curves in their downward trek. The private place between her legs tightened. She couldn't believe it when he reached her stomach. The warmth of his palm penetrated the fabric of her dress and petticoat. He inched her dress upward.

"Good Lord," she breathed when cool air washed over her legs—then her thighs. "This is not proper."

"Nae, my lady, it isn't," he murmured against her breast.

His fingers brushed her thigh and she started.

He lifted his head an inch from her breast and said, "I will not hurt you."

Hurt her? That she didn't fear. It was the riotous feelings flooding her.

His fingers reached her abdomen and she tensed. He drew slow, light circles. The tension in her shoulders eased, though she couldn't think past the flick of his tongue against her nipple. What was he doing? Her mind snapped onto the finger that slipped into the curls below her belly button. She drew a stuttered breath as the digit dipped into the moist heat and brushed her sex.

Chastity drew a sharp breath when he gently massaged her. Sweet God, he was casting some sort of spell on her. She understood well enough how to pleasure herself—but she hadn't known a man could make her feel this way. Desire streaked through her when he flicked his tongue against her nipple as he massaged her faster. She buried her face in his neck and breathed deep of his scent. Her head spun and she couldn't refrain from arching into his finger. A sudden tide of pleasure washed over her. Chastity cried out and light flashed beneath her eyelids.

Her mind registered his groan and she vaguely wondered how she would ever look him in the eye again.

❧

A SHORT WHILE LATER, SIR STIRLING KEPT CHASTITY CLOSE AT his side as they walked from the carriage toward Gledstone Hall. Once out of earshot of the driver, he said, "I assume we would do better to enter through the kitchen?"

She nodded, and he veered right. They continued around the house to the rear door. He allowed her to precede him up the four steps and into the empty kitchen. They were lucky that Cook wasn't up yet.

He grasped her arm and turned her to face him. "Can I trust you to stay here and not venture out again?"

"Can I trust you not to fight duels?" she countered.

He grinned and she resisted the urge to smile back. The man's humor was contagious.

"You must trust me on this, Chastity. I know what I'm doing."

"If you are shot—"

"Your problems will be solved," he cut in. His eyes twinkled.

Her cheeks flushed hot, but embarrassment gave way to pique. "This is exactly what I feared. You will laugh at me every time we speak."

"I am not laughing at you, love. I am wooing you."

She blinked. "Wooing? You look for every opportunity to drive me to distraction."

"Exactly," he said, and before she realized his intent, he pushed her against the wall and pressed his body against hers.

He kissed her and her head spun at the press of his hard length against her abdomen. He broke the kiss, then turned and strode the three paces to the door. He reached the first step, then paused in closing the door, and said, "Do not force me into action by gainsaying me in this matter, Chastity. Contrary to what you think, I will not be your jailer. But neither will I allow you to interfere in matters that you know nothing of. I will see you at the church later today." He gave her no chance to reply, but closed the door.

Chastity stared at the door. Good Lord. With her mind on the duel, she'd forgotten that she was to marry in a few hours.

CHAPTER 6

AFTER STIRLING RETURNED TO DORRING'S MANSION AND assured himself the coward really had fled, he took John back to Gledstone Hall, then stayed parked outside the mansion, until he spotted the duke's carriage rounding the house, headed for the main door. He half feared his bride would still attempt to flee, but he didn't want to chance her knowing he'd kept watch the entire night.

He now awaited her at the altar as her sisters' grooms had and, to his surprise, he found himself nervous. It seemed he waited forever, and he laughed at the realization that no groom found it easy to await his bride.

The parson fidgeted. The man was probably tired of marrying Roxburgh daughters. Fortunately, this would be his last. The minister's eyes shifted past Stirling and he tensed. The duke and Chastity must have entered the church. He released a slow breath, then turned in anticipation of hearing the music begin as the two began the walk up the aisle. He started at sight of the duke striding toward him alone.

Stirling hurried forward and they met halfway down the

aisle. "Chastity is nowhere to be found," he whispered to Stirling.

"Bloody hell," Stirling cursed under his breath. They strode from the chapel into the foyer. "When did you last see her?" he demanded.

"Her sisters left her in the small parlor. That was only ten minutes ago."

"She can't have gone far," he said. "You gather your daughters' husbands and fan them out. I'll start looking for her."

The duke nodded and Stirling hurried from the chapel out into the overcast day. He paused at the bottom of the steps. Where would she have gone? Carriages and horses awaited out front and around the side of the church. She would probably want to avoid being seen by the drivers, so would likely have headed east.

Stirling hurried around the side of the church toward the woods that bordered the river. She only had to walk a quarter mile to reach a small inn. There, she could rent a horse. Damn her, did she truly despise marriage—and him—so much that she would run away like this? His chest tightened. He had been certain he could make her fall in love with him. Last night, he'd been sure she had begun to thaw. Had he miscalculated in making love to her? She clearly had little or no experience, but she had been receptive to him. He was sure of it.

He plunged into the woods and hurried along a narrow path. Should he rethink their marriage? If she truly shunned marriage this much— Could he let her go? He looked up from the path and saw her descending the gentle slope near the water. He started. Was she going to throw herself into the river?

Stirling broke into a run. He leapt over a fallen log and didn't quite manage to miss a branch that whacked him across the leg. He dodged a large tree. She neared the river. Should he call out to her? Might she jump if she saw him? He pumped his legs faster. She abruptly turned and faced him. He discerned the confusion on her face. She froze, and in two more heartbeats he reached her side and yanked her to him.

She cried out and caught him off guard with a kick to his shin. They toppled to the ground and he hugged her close as they rolled toward the water. A rock scraped his knuckle and he cursed. He tried to change their course, but only managed to turn so that their heads would hit the water first. With one mighty yank, he turned them again and they struck the water feet first.

With one hand, he held Chastity close and grabbed for brush that overhung the river. His fingers slid along bark, slicing his flesh, but he prevented them from being swept down river. Chastity clung to his neck, sputtering.

"Hold tight," he ordered.

"Even if it means drowning you," she snapped.

That was something. Tentatively, Stirling loosened his hold. Her arms remained tightly wound around his neck. He grabbed the bush with his free hand and began hauling them up the bank. When his feet hit the river bottom, he pulled her up until she could walk, as well. He dragged her up and over the bank and rolled away from the river's edge. They lay panting for several moments, wet, muddy and out of breath.

Chastity abruptly pushed onto her knees and pummeled his chest with her fists. "Have you completely lost your mind? What is wrong with you?"

He sat upright and seized her wrists. "Wrong with me?" His gaze caught on her dress. The damned thing was near indecent, wet and clinging to her breasts like a second skin. She tried to yank free of his grasp. He yanked his gaze to her face.

"Why did you run away?"

"What are you talking about? I was taking a short walk before—" She broke off.

He narrowed his eyes. "Before you were to walk the plank, eh, lass?"

Chastity yanked free of him and tried to stand. Her dress tangled her legs and she tripped. She cried out and started to slide down the bank. Stirling seized her arm and shoved to his feet as he hauled her over his shoulder.

"You have gone mad," she growled.

"Of that there is no doubt," he muttered, and strode up the bank and through the woods.

Chastity kicked and pounded his back with her fists. The wench managed a couple of hard blows to his ribs. He couldn't stop a grunt and she gave a dark laugh that made him wonder about both their sanities.

"You will pay for this," she cried when they neared the church.

"Indeed, I shall," he replied.

The duke emerged from the woods on the opposite side of the church, followed by three other men. He broke into a run and met them at the church steps.

"What in God's name happened?"

"We fell in the river," Stirling shot back. He stomped up the steps and threw back the door, then strode inside the church foyer with Chastity slung over his shoulder.

"Put me down!" she shouted.

He ignored her.

"Don't you dare go into the chapel with me over your shoulder and us dripping wet," she warned.

Stirling marched through the open doors and up the aisle.

Many of the guests surged to their feet. Uproarious laughter filled the small chapel.

"Ohhh," Chastity growled, and Stirling was sure she was trying to bite his back.

"Sir," a man called, and the vicar hurried past Stirling, then turned to face him. Stirling didn't stop, which forced the man to walk backwards. "Oh dear," the man said. "Perhaps you should put your fiancée down."

Stirling caught sight of Chastity's sisters standing near their seats in the front pew. All three sisters' eyes were wide and their husbands had their arms about their waists.

Stirling reached the podium and said, "Get on with it, Minister."

The man's eyes widened and more laughter went up amongst the guests. "You must set her down," he said.

"There is no law that says the bride must be standing," Stirling said.

"I will not marry you this way," Chastity shot back.

Her father arrived at Stirling's side. "Ye returned home last night at four in the morning with Sir Stirling in a rented coach," he said. "The minister's vows are a mere formality."

She gasped. "You told him!"

More laughter from the guests.

"I did not," Stirling said. "But you just did. Minister, say the vows or we will go straight to the wedding bed now."

"You mustn't do that, sir," he said.

"Then do your dirty work now," Stirling ordered.

"I will not consent." Chastity began to thrash.

Stirling clamped one arm over her legs and gave her bottom a swat.

She cried out—and he was sure he heard her sisters gasp amongst the uproar that followed.

"Get on with it, Minister."

The vicar stuttered through the vows so badly that Stirling wondered if they held any validity at all. Chastity tried to twist free, but Stirling gave her another swat, this one a bit harder. She howled in what he was sure was more rage than pain, and threatened to call the legions from hell to punish him. When the vicar asked if Stirling took her to wife, he said, "God have mercy upon my soul, aye. I take her."

"You will need mercy," she muttered darkly.

When the minister asked her to repeat the vows, she went quiet. Stirling said in a low voice, "Either repeat your vows, Chastity, or I will put you into the first carriage we find outside and consummate our marriage with everyone listening to your cries of pleasure."

She gasped. "You fiend."

"A fiend who knows how to please you, madam. Repeat the vows or we begin with a kiss right here at the altar that will be more indecent than you can imagine. Do you take me for your husband?" he demanded.

"For better or worse," she said. "Guess which one you will get?"

"I am aware of my fate." He looked at the minister. "Are we finished?"

He looked confused. "The rings."

"A mere formality. Where is the damned registry?"

The man hurried to the book lying left of the altar. Stirling followed. Chastity tried to kick, and his signature came out as shaky as an old man's.

He looked at the duke. "Your Grace, would you lift the book so my wife can sign?"

"I will not sign," she muttered.

"The carriage awaits us, Chastity," Stirling warned.

The duke hefted the big book up and Stirling turned so that Chastity faced it. She went stiff.

"Sign," the duke said, "or I will annul the marriage and marry you to Lord Bigly."

"What?" she cried. "What of Lord Hathaway?"

"He is too good for you. Lord Bigly is older and certainly more reprehensible to you."

"You are a traitor," she cried, and grabbed the quill from him.

She signed with a jerky motion and Stirling didn't wait for

anything more, but strode from the chapel, with her rigid over his shoulder. He emerged from the church and hurried down the steps to the nearest carriage.

"Excuse me, sir," the driver called when he opened the door, "but I'm waiting for Mrs. MacPherson."

"She gave me leave to borrow her carriage. Begin to drive, *now*."

"Where to, sir?"

"Stay in the country." Stirling tossed Chastity onto the seat and vaulted inside. A cheer went up as he pulled the door shut.

She glared at him in the dim light. "Stay on your side of the coach," she warned. "I married you, so you have no reason to carry out your threat to-to—" She growled in frustration.

The carriage started forward with a squeaky wheel and a clop of horses' hooves on stone.

He stared back. "Do not play the injured miss with me. We are not parked outside the church, so no one will be privy to our lovemaking."

Her mouth fell open. "You forced me to marry you—"

"Forced you? I beg to differ," he said on a laugh. "This entire scheme was your idea."

She started to reply, then glared.

"Why did you run away?" he demanded.

"I didn't. I went for a walk."

"You expect me to believe that?" he said.

Her eyes narrowed. "Wouldn't you want to clear your head if you were going to marry *you*?"

Stirling blinked. How did he respond to that logic?

The carriage jostled over a bump. "When have I ever hesitated to tell you what I thought?" she demanded.

She had a point. Good God, he was a bigger fool than the three men he had married to her sisters. He thought she had run and he'd nearly lost his mind.

"I thought I'd lost you," he whispered.

She frowned. "What?"

"I saw you walking so near the river…"

Chastity stared. "You thought I intended to end my life? You think well of yourself if you think I'd kill myself over you."

"You have fought marrying me from the start. How was I to think anything different?"

"I would brain you in your sleep before I would end my own life." She shook her head. "My God, does becoming the Duke of Roxburgh mean so much to you that you would risk your life by jumping in the river to save me?"

He scowled. "If you recall, I didn't jump in to save you." To his shock, she laughed.

"Nae, you fool. You threw me to the ground and dragged me down with you."

Stirling stared. She truly was magnificent. How many women would take a man to task for practically attacking them —then laugh at him? "That will teach you to leave our wedding day—and to walk too near the river."

"And it will teach you not to underestimate me. Do you really believe that if I wanted to run away that I would get only as far as the river?" She rolled her eyes.

"How far would you have gone?"

She swayed as the carriage made a slight turn. "If I told you that, then I could never go there, could I?"

He fought to hide a grin. "I shall have to keep a close eye on you."

"Like you did last night?"

She knew?

"Last night?" he repeated.

"Spare me the innocent looks." She pinned him with a stare. "You have married my sisters to good men. Thank you."

Stirling blinked. "I beg your pardon?"

"Don't act so surprised. I might not want to marry you, but that doesn't mean I don't appreciate what you did for them."

"How do you feel about being married to me? Surely, I've proven myself to be of *some* use."

Her cheeks flushed and he longed to see that blush while he moved inside her.

"*Use*, as in when you tried to drown me?" she said.

He shrugged. "I did save you, as well."

"With a savior like you, who needs enemies?"

"I can see I need to redeem myself."

Her face clouded in confusion—then her eyes widened and he felt certain she was attempting to melt into the seat. He recognized her embarrassment and perhaps a little apprehension, but no hatred for him, and certainly no loathing for what he'd done to her last night. In fact, he would wager another good ship that she would let him do it to her again. A light patter of rain began to beat down on the carriage. In truth, he was about to wager something far more important.

His heart.

CHAPTER 7

CHASTITY TAMPED DOWN HER RISING PANIC. SHE WAS MARRIED. Not just married. Married to a very handsome, very intelligent man. A dangerous man. A man who could make her lose her sanity. He would take her body, and eventually her soul. That, she'd sworn after eloping with Lord Everston, would never happen again. Love was well and good, but losing oneself wasn't. Since she had no intention of giving all of herself to a man, she'd seen no reason to marry.

But this man would take all she had, then demand more. The look in his eyes confirmed her thoughts. Only an hour ago, he'd nearly killed her—killed them both. Yet he stared at her boldly, demanding that she give what he wanted and take what he offered: pleasure.

He startled her by moving to the seat beside her.

"Use some sense," she said. "We are not in your private bedchamber. This is a public coach."

"This is a private carriage, if I am not mistaken. That aside, being in a public coach did not hinder you last night."

"It should have," she muttered, and the rogue laughed.

"On the contrary, my lady, it is good for you." Before she could argue, he dragged her across his lap. "Let me demonstrate."

He crushed her to him and kissed her so soundly that she wondered if she'd ever truly been kissed before. Chastity found herself back against the cushion, him half on top of her, his wicked hand tugging down her bodice, then cupping her breast. His tongue gently—but insistent—slipped past her lips and he thrust in and out in a fashion that heated her and made her head spin.

The hard ridge that pressed against her abdomen caught her attention and she half feared—and half hoped—he would demand his husbandly rights that very instant. She started when he laid his palm on her leg. Warmth seeped through the cold, wet fabric of her dress to her skin. She shivered as much from his touch as the thought that he might stroke her as he had last night. Merciful heaven, the man was a warlock. He sucked her tongue into his mouth and lay more heavily on her, pressing her deeper into the cushion. He gave a low laugh and she realized he'd read her mind. It was just as she feared: he would quickly own her.

"You tempt me, Lady Chastity," he whispered.

Her mind muddled. What did he mean?

"Ask for anything, and it's yours."

What was he talking about? She didn't understand. But she did understand that he was tugging the hem of her dress upward.

"I swear to make you happy," he said.

He grasped her hand and drew it to him. Her palm covered his erection.

"Sir," she cried, and tried to yank her hand free.

"Nae, Chastity. We are married. You need not fear that this is wrong."

Wrong? It felt oddly right. But the feelings flooded her and she couldn't make sense of anything. He abruptly sat up and pulled her across his lap again. He was breathing heavily, his chest rising and falling.

"Bloody hell," he muttered. "I cannot tumble you like a common tavern wench—especially on our wedding day."

"You already did," she said.

He gave a strangled laugh. "Not quite, love, but I came damned close."

"It's what you threatened to do," she said.

"By God," he exclaimed. "You make it sound as though that's what you want."

Chastity flushed. He was right—and she felt like a tavern wench.

He muttered something under his breath, then slid her from his lap. He stripped off his coat and had his falls unbuttoned in an instant. His erection sprang free and Chastity swallowed.

Sir Stirling laid her back on the cushion and pulled her dress up to her waist. He lowered himself onto her and she expected him to immediately drive his cock into her. Instead, he levered up onto his elbows and kissed her. Chastity grasped his forearms. Muscles strained beneath her fingers. His kiss remained gentle as he eased her legs apart. The carriage bounced over ruts and his manhood bumped her stomach. He drew in a sharp breath, then eased her bottom closer to the edge of the cushion. She realized he had braced one knee on the floor.

He probed her opening with the head of his rod as he traced the seam of her mouth with his tongue. Chastity released a breath—then tensed when he suddenly thrust inside her, hilt deep.

He stilled, his breathing ragged. "Why didn't you tell me?"

There hadn't been any pain as she expected, but he felt strange and impossibly large inside her.

"Chastity."

She jarred. "What?"

He lifted higher on his elbows and looked down on her. "You didn't tell me you were a virgin."

She became aware of the clop of the horses as the coach picked up pace. She sighed. The mood was ruined. "Wouldn't it be more logical that I would have told you if I wasn't a virgin?"

"I'm surprised you didn't lie to me, in hopes of discouraging me," he said.

"Lord, I didn't think of it. But I doubt it would have worked. I would have tried, though."

He laughed. Then he stopped laughing and began to move inside her. The mood, she realized with a gasp, wasn't so ruined after all. Chastity couldn't believe the sweet sensations that rippled through her. He moved slowly, which seemed to her some sort of torture. The carriage jolted and it felt as if he'd speared her very womb. Pleasure spiked. He groaned and moved faster.

"Goodness," she breathed.

"Relax, love, and let me please you."

How much more could he please her? She felt ready to burst.

"Do you like this?" He thrust deep.

She drew a sharp breath.

"I'll take that as a yes." He thrust deep again and increased his speed.

Her head began to whirl. Sir Stirling rolled onto the seat, keeping her joined with him, then scooted so that she lay on top of him. Chastity froze.

"Sit up," he said.

"What?"

"Sit up."

He gently pushed her into a sitting position. His cock almost slipped out, but he reached between them and held himself steady as she repositioned herself. Embarrassment washed over her when they made eye contact.

"No need to be embarrassed," he said. "Move up and down on me as it pleases you."

She yanked her eyes to his face. "That is-is indecent."

He gave a hoarse laugh. "Not by half, love." He grasped her bottom and gently lifted her. Chastity quickly braced her palms on his chest. He lowered her, then lifted her again. After a few strokes she was startled by the pleasant friction between them.

"Find the position that best suits you," he whispered.

She leaned forward slightly and after three strokes had to admit the sensations were amazing. He lifted and brought her down on him faster and harder. His breath came harder. The sounds made her stomach clench. She recognized the oncoming orgasm, but couldn't believe the feelings originating deep inside.

Pleasure swept through her. She cried out and dropped her head onto his chest as he arched his hips, stroking, driving deeper inside her as the orgasm rolled over her with more intensity. His fingers tightened on her buttocks and he groaned as he slowed his strokes, once, twice, then a third and fourth time before he relaxed.

Chastity went limp. He wrapped his arms around her and stroked her hair. She felt oddly content and wondered if he felt any of the same. At last, he slowly slipped out of her and she relaxed on top of him. She released a breath, her body strangely weary and sated. Unexpectedly, she recalled his words to her father. *"I can deal with Dorring. There is no need to worry the lass."* He'd defended and even protected her against her father's ire. Her father was a good man, and would never truly hurt her. Still, no one other than her father had ever protected her against anyone or anything. Knowing she'd tricked him, he'd put himself between her and her father and he hadn't demonstrated any rancor toward her for playing him false. Why had he done that?

His arms tightened around her. "I promise, next time will be better," he said, and her mind said, *Dangerous, dangerous, dangerous.*

CHAPTER 8

CHASTITY COULDN'T HAVE BEEN MORE WRONG ABOUT MARRIED life...and her family. She had expected her sisters to go their separate ways, and had thought that she would be lucky to see them on occasional holidays. Lucy spent at least two days a week as Gledstone. Olivia's husband worked closely with Stirling on a new shipping venture they'd formed, which meant he and Olivia hadn't returned to Lossiemouth as he'd originally planned. He'd agreed to give up the rented townhouse, for a twenty minute ride was too much—so the men said—for them to work the late nights they had planned. And Jessica, well, Jessica had taken to running her husband's estate, Baldain House, with such gusto that she constantly called upon Chastity for help and advice.

As had become their custom on Sunday afternoons, they all sat in the parlor after the afternoon meal, the men playing chess while Lucy and Olivia watched. Jessica sat with Chastity on the divan near the hearth. Today, a guest quietly talked business with Stirling in the chairs near the open balcony doors. Stirling looked up and Chastity resisted the urge to yank her gaze away when his eyes locked with hers. He had an uncanny way of knowing when she was looking at him. Or maybe he was simply arrogant enough to know she was too-often looking at him. A smile curved his mouth and she figured the answer was the latter: the man was confident. He knew she belonged to him heart, body, and soul.

"Have you told him yet?" Jessica asked.

Chastity broke from her thoughts and looked at her sisters. "What?"

"Have you told him you're expecting a baby?"

Chastity started. "What—how did you know?"

Jessica's eyes sparkled. "Because I am going to have a baby, too."

Tears sprang to her eyes. "Oh, Jessica." They hugged, and from the corner of her eye, Chastity saw the curious look on her husband's face. She forced back tears as she and Jessica separated.

Jessica said, "I haven't told Patrick yet. I plan to do so when we return home today."

Chastity nodded, unable to speak.

"Oh dear, here comes trouble." Jessica laughed.

Chastity looked up. Stirling was striding toward them. Trouble, was right.

"I think I'll leave you to your ogre," Jessica whispered.

"Jessica," Chastity hissed, but her sister only pressed a kiss to her cheek before hurrying away.

Stirling reached her and lowered himself onto the divan beside her. "Your sister seems in especially good humor today."

Chastity gave him a narrow-eyed look, but said nothing.

He lifted a brow. "Is there an announcement in the offing?"

Of course, he knew. He seemed to know everything—well, almost everything. He didn't yet know the topic of her announcement.

"What business were you and Lord Benton discussing?" she asked.

"The young lordling is experiencing a bit of a dilemma," he replied. "He is in love with a certain young lady who seems not to know he exists."

"What—never say you are playing marriage maker again?" She rolled her eyes. "Good Lord."

He gave a careless shrug, but she glimpsed the twinkle in his eye. "I have come to have a soft spot in my heart for seeing true love prevail."

"More like, you enjoy dabbling in others' lives," she said.

"They do make it easy." He leaned back against the cushion. "Unlike you, wife, who I am still trying to figure out."

"Rubbish," she said. "You are certain you have me figured out."

He grunted. "Hardly. Though I have figured out that we will have a child in less than eight months."

She started. "But how did you know?"

His eyes gleamed with satisfaction. "A man notices certain changes in his wife's body—when he pays attention."

To her chagrin, she couldn't halt the warmth that spread up her cheeks.

"No need to be embarrassed, my dear."

He always said that, but she too often was embarrassed. He had a knack for making her stomach do somersaults.

"Are you happy?" he asked.

"That is an odd question."

"On the contrary, I think it is a perfectly normal question. Are you happy we are going to have a child?"

She was. Chastity nodded. "I am."

He smiled and her treacherous stomach did a somersault. "If we have a son, my father will be relieved that the title is safe."

"Oh, I think he isn't the least bit worried on that account," Stirling said.

Chastity nodded. "With all of us married, he is certain to have a male heir at some point."

"He may very well have a male heir of his own."

She frowned. "What are you talking about?"

"There is a certain widow who has taken an interest in the duke."

Chastity stared. "What? Who is she? Oh, I imagine she is after his title. I must meet this woman. How long has this been going on?"

He laughed. "Now, who is it that likes dabbling in others' lives?"

"This isn't dabbling," she shot back. "My father is a man, and men are easily swayed by a pretty face. If she is a fortune hunter—"

"I assure you, she is no fortune hunter."

Then she understood. "My God, you found him a match?" She couldn't believe it.

"I only introduced them," he said. "Your father did the rest."

Chastity shifted her attention to her father. He hadn't said a word. "I must meet her."

"In due time, Chastity. For now, give them a chance to get to know one another."

"Are you saying he truly might remarry?" she demanded.

"Why not? He isn't old."

"You can't be in favor of him marrying. If he has a son, you won't become the Duke of Roxburgh."

He locked eyes with her. "I never planned on becoming his heir."

"But that's why you married me."

He angled his head. "Whatever gave you that idea?"

"Well—what else could it be?"

He held her gaze. "Love."

"Love? You never mentioned love before."

"You wouldn't have believed me."

He was right.

"Now, I have no reason to lie," he said.

She didn't know what to say.

"Surely, I haven't left you speechless?" Stirling teased. "This is a rarity. I tell you what, why don't you just admit you love me and be done with it?"

"Love you?" she whispered.

He gave a single nod. "It's all right, sweetheart. There's no need to be embarrassed. Tell you what, I'll say it first."

Her heart began to pound hard.

He took her hand and lifted it to his lips. Eyes locked with hers, he brushed his mouth against her knuckles, then whispered, "I love you."

She stared.

"It's all right," he said. "I said it first. You're in no danger of losing your heart to a man who hasn't already lost his to you."

"You're insane," she whispered.

"That is a well-established fact," he said. "But it is not what we are discussing. Can you deny that you love me?"

She shook her head and he flashed a heart-stopping smile.

"Good."

He waited.

Did she love him? She did. And she said so.

SNEAK PEEK AT ONE GOOD GENTLEMAN

One Good Gentleman
The Marriage Maker
Book Five
Rules of Refinement

Summer Hanford

Her virtue or her dreams . . . which must she abandon?

Emilia Glasbarr doesn't want to be a country miss with a yard full of geese and a scant handful of neighbors. She wants the music, theatre and art found in Scotland's capital city. She's sunk her every resource into finishing school to find a city-dwelling husband. Unfortunately, the only man interested wants her for a far less savory purpose.

CHAPTER 1

At the end of each season, Lady Peddington's School for Young Ladies threw not one, or even two, but four balls over the course of four weeks. If a young woman couldn't meet the man of her dreams in that length of time, well, she'd best hope a man awaited her at home because four was the schools' more than generous limit. To Miss Emilia Glasbarr's dismay, the first of these balls was stuttering to an end, and she still lacked a suitor.

Emilia huddled near the refreshments table and tried to untangle the scene before her. Many of the girls, certainly the ones already spoken for, had retired for the evening. Those who remained, behaved with a lack of propriety that Emilia found moderately shocking. Gloves were removed. Laughter, not polite titters, sounded. Footmen had appeared to snuff out most of the candles, leaving the vast ballroom enshrouded in flickering half-light. Most disconcerting, the few instructors who still chaperone turned a blind eye. Only Emilia's desperation not to live out the remainder of her days as a country Miss kept her there. Normally, she would retreat from such a scene.

A waltz began and Emilia stifled a gasp. No respectable young woman danced the waltz. They'd been taught as much at the very school in which she stood. Gentlemen reached out, clasped ladies close. Distressed by the bedlam before her, Emilia turned away from the whirling figures. She swallowed, her throat dry, and reached for a glass of punch.

The gulp she took burned the whole way down, laced with some strong spirit. She raised incredulous eyes to the woman who oversaw the punch table, their etiquette instructor, and received a wink. Disconcerted, Emilia set out around the edge of the room, unsure what to do with the glass she held. Putting the punch down now would be ill-mannered, but she dared not drink more. The one gulp already left her dizzy.

A gentleman strode toward her. Emilia dropped her gaze demurely. She knew who he was, for the school kept minia-tures of all the local nobility, and she knew he wasn't there to find a wife. He was already wed. She could only assume he came to support the school, to help Lady Peddington's students practice the art of dancing at a real social engagement, not under the eyes of an instructor.

She suppressed a sigh of disappointment that an eligible gentleman refused to appear, for well-bred ladies didn't sigh, and angled toward the wall to give him room to pass without interfering with the dancers. She stopped in surprise when he stepped in front of her. His too-strong cologne assailed her nostrils. Punch sloshed onto her gloved fingers. Her face heated at her clumsiness.

His eyes dipped toward the glass for a moment. "Partaking of Lady Peddington's famous midnight punch, I see." His accent was urbane. Dark eyes looked down at her from under oiled brown hair.

"Midnight punch?" she repeated, confused.

"No need to play coy. I love Lady Peddington's special

midnight brew, and a girl who drinks it." He leaned forward as he spoke and used his six inches of superior height to look down the front of her white muslin gown.

Emilia's blush deepened. "I've only taken one sip." She almost choked on her own inanity, but what was one to say to that statement, or that look? He wasn't behaving the way they'd been taught men should behave, let alone married members of the peerage.

"You should drink up then, dear girl." He wrapped a hand around hers and lifted the glass to her lips.

Emilia was too shocked by his hand on hers to protest. She gagged as the heavily laced punch tumbled into her mouth. She choked it down, for one could hardly spit up on a viscount.

"That's better," he said when the glass was empty. He dabbed at the corners of her mouth with a glove-encased thumb.

Emilia watched him through eyes as wide as saucers. "My lord," she managed to gasp out.

His smile was pleased. "So, you know who I am?"

"Indeed, I do, Lord Ailbeart, but I'm sure we've never met, and certainly do no' know each other well enough for you to put your hands on me."

He raised thick eyebrows. "Don't we? Perhaps you would care for a bit more punch?"

"I most certainly would not." Already the room had begun a gentle spin. Emilia rarely tasted wine, and had eaten lightly, nervous for the dance. Whatever was in the punch, and she suspected scotch, had gone straight to her head.

Far from appearing offended by her rejoinder, the viscount grinned. His fingers grazed her cheek as he tugged on one of her yellow curls before letting it spring back into place. "Spirited, aren't you? I want a spirited mistress this time. The last one was too well trained. A lady can be too polished."

Emilia was doubly upset she'd consumed the punch, for she had nothing to throw in his face. "Did I hear you suggest I be your mistress, my lord?" she gritted out. She hadn't spent her entire dowry on finishing school to become this man's plaything.

"I knew I'd picked a good one in you." His grin was smug.

Emilia glared through narrowed hazel eyes. "Picked?"

"Aye. I told the other fellows, stay clear of that golden-haired beauty. She's mine." He spoke in a warm, almost sweet tone, as if praising a favored pet. His gaze roamed over her.

Emilia drew in a harsh breath, too offended to be embarrassed. "I do not believe that is for you to say, my lord."

"But it is, and since I have, no one else will dare dance with you." He closed the distance between them, his voice low and suddenly edged with malice. "And when you find yourself all alone at the end of the fourth ball, with the choice of a fine house in the heart of Edinburgh or slogging back to whatever obscure corner of the countryside you crawled in from, you'll realize that being my most prized possession is more desirable."

He grabbed the back of her neck, yanked her forward and kissed her. It was a brief, rough kiss that left her reeling as he sauntered away. Emilia was aghast. She jerked her gaze around the room, but no one seemed to have noticed. Mortified, breath ragged, she fled the ballroom.

Emilia clutched her skirt in both hands to keep the hem off the floor and ran through the dim halls of Lady Peddington's School. The stench of Viscount Dunreid's cologne clung to her. She didn't know where she went until she burst through the door to the drawing classroom, the room where she always felt happiest. To her relief, Missus Millview, the drawing instructor, was there.

"Miss Glasbarr?" Missus Millview rose from her chair.

"Whatever is the matter? What are you doing here? It's well after midnight."

She stumbled across the room toward her instructor. "Lord Ailbeart, that is, Viscount Dunreid kissed me," she blurted. "I didnae want him to, but he did." She burst into tears.

Missus Millview reached her side and wrapped Emilia in a warm embrace. "There, there, my dear child," she murmured. "You shouldn't be up after midnight. You aren't the sort. There's been an error."

Emilia sniffed. "An error?" Did midnight signify in some way? "I don't understand."

Missus Millview shook her head, eyes sympathetic in her long face. "It's nothing, child, nothing at all. Only that you should retire earlier at the next ball, to avoid this sort of thing. Gentlemen tend to get out of hand in the later hours."

"They do?" Emilia pulled away. She wiped at her cheeks with the heels of her hands.

"Of course." Missus Millview gave her a gentle smile. "You dance the early dances from now on and retire before midnight, and forget this incident with Lord Ailbeart ever occurred."

"But I can't," Emilia cried. "No one will dance with me. Not one gentleman asked. Lord Ailbeart said he warned them away because I'm to be...to be..." She couldn't say it aloud, what he'd propositioned. "What am I to do? I convinced my parents to let me use the money they set aside for my dowry to come here. I told them a man would prefer a cultured bride over one with a small sum. I don't want to go back to the country. I want to stay here where there is music and art."

Missus Millview's brow creased, her look one of compassion. Emilia glanced around the nearly dark room. Why was Missus Ailbeart in her classroom at that hour? She took in the desk. The scattered candle stubs illuminated receipts and pages filled with rows of numbers.

Missus Millview followed her gaze. She let out a sigh, and passed a hand over tired eyes. "Yes, we must all worry about our funds, child."

Concern of another sort stole through Emilia. Missus Millview was a good person, and her favorite instructor. "Is there anything I can do?"

"Do?" Missus Millview shook her head. "No. I'll be well enough, so long as I keep my place here." She pressed her lips into a tight frown and dragged her gaze from her desk, back to Emilia. "I should like to help you, child. You aren't one who should have been brought to Lord Ailbeart's attention. I suspect it's your beauty that's the trouble, not that you can help that."

Emilia blinked. Beauty? She knew she had no obvious flaws in appearance, but she hardly thought she had sufficient beauty to garner attention, especially from a viscount. "You can help me?" Her voice caught at the hope that surged within her.

Missus Millview looked to her pages of numbers again. She gave a sharp nod. "I can, but you must promise not to tell any of the other girls. I can't lose my place here. I'm not young or beautiful enough to make my way if I do."

"I promise," Emilia said eagerly. "Please, what can I do? I simply want to marry a kind man. I do no' need a title, or wealth, or much of anything, really. Just a gentleman who lives in the city."

"You won't tell those three friends of yours?" Missus Millview eyed her shrewdly. "I know how inseparable you four are, and I suspect they may be in the same boat. You must promise not to tell them what I'll reveal to you, child. I've come to care for you, but a woman alone in this world must look out for herself."

Emilia bit back a hasty acceptance. Her friends had all retired earlier as, apparently, proper young women did. They'd been discouraged as they'd also lacked admirers. Could she consign any of them to men like Lord Ailbeart?

She drew in a breath. She couldn't, but she would find a way to help without breaking Missus Millview's confidence. "I promise I won't tell the other girls, even my friends."

Missus Millview offered a relieved smile. "Well then, this should help you." She crossed to the desk, then pulled free a clean page and began to write.

Emilia followed her. She looked over Missus Millview's shoulder to take in the elegantly penned address and a name. "Sir Stirling James," she read aloud.

Missus Millview turned to offer the page. "Yes. They call him The Marriage Maker. If anyone can help you, he can." Her face went stern, as it did when Emilia attempted anything less than her best work. "But don't forget your promise."

"I won't, Missus Millview." Emilia folded the page in half. "Thank you."

"You're a good child," Missus Millview said. "Too good for the likes of Viscount Dunreid. Can you reach your chamber well enough?"

Emilia thought about the empty halls. No one had stopped her on her way to the classroom. She nodded. "I can." She gave Missus Millview a quick hug. "Thank you. You've saved me, and I won't tell the others."

Missus Millview sighed and shook her head. "I hope not, child, I truly do."

Emilia left with a lighter heart than she'd had in hours. She took the back way to her room, thankful the halls and stairs were as blissfully empty as she'd hoped. As she walked, she formulated a plan. She would write this Sir Stirling James now, before bed. She would tell him of her plight, and include a small portrait she'd done of herself, on the chance she really was as pretty as Missus Millview said.

In fact, she would include portraits of her three friends as well, and beg him to help them all. Missus Millview had made her swear not to tell any of the other girls about Sir Stirling James. That didn't mean Emilia couldn't tell him about them. She smiled as she reached the safety of her room and lit a candle, pleased with her plan.

CHAPTER 2

ROBERT BANBROOK SAT ALONE AT A TABLE IN HIS CLUB, STARING into a half-empty glass of scotch. The only good thing about Scotland, as far as he was concerned. One up, then, on England. The Irish had Irish Whiskey, the Scots had Scottish Whisky. What did England offer a man to drown his sorrows? Gin. Robert shuddered at the thought. He swallowed the rest of the glass to dispel the memory of the revolting stuff.

"You look a bit peaked there, Banbrook," a jovial voice said. A large hand clasped his shoulder briefly.

Robert looked up from his empty tumbler and squinted to bring Sir Stirling James into focus. Stirling pulled out a chair and seated himself at the table.

"I'm as fine as a fiddle, Stirling, I can assure you." Robert reached for the nearly empty decanter before him. He missed once, but claimed it on the second try. He flashed Stirling a grin, proud of his success. "You see? Fine as a fiddle," Robert repeated.

Liquid sloshed onto his fingers and he looked down. Whisky tumbled from the mouth of the crystal decanter and over the hand clasping the tumbler. Furrowing his brow in concentration, he angled the bottle to get more into the glass.

"I'm glad to hear it, Banbrook, because I was worried you'd spent the past three days in this club drinking yourself to death." Stirling lifted an arm and waved. A footman hurried over with a cloth to sop up the spilled liquor.

"Oh, I have. I am." Robert offered a grin, though he could hardly feel his face.

"I take it this ill-conceived effort has to do with a certain young lady?" Stirling asked as the footman mopped the spill.

"You, Geoffrey, bring me another bottle," Robert said to the footman. He turned back to Stirling. "You use the word *lady* loosely."

"I find that doubtful." Stirling nodded toward the footman. "John will ignore your request." Stirling emphasized the man's name. "The entire staff will. I've had you cut off."

Robert let out a mumbled curse. The footman departed without looking at him. A glance showed no others near.

"Can't you leave me to drink myself to death in peace?" Robert asked. He squinted at the older gentleman. "You used to be fun." He knocked back his drink and realized very little whisky had made its way into his glass.

"Oh, I have something fun planned, never fear." Stirling stood and gestured again.

Footsteps sounded behind Robert. He craned his neck in an effort to see who approached. Two of the burlier footmen, their faces set, marched toward him. Or was there one and he was seeing the man twice? He blinked several times, but neither of the two disappeared.

Large hands clasped his arms and lifted him from the chair. At least four hands, so at least two of the fellows, then. Or was that three? The empty tumbler slipped free of his grasp to hit the table with a thunk.

The sound drew his attention as the men got him to his feet.

Sad empty tumbler. All it wanted was to do its duty by him. So loyal. Not like women.

Stirling appeared at his side, swaying like a storm-tossed schooner. "What do you think, Banbrook, can you walk?"

Robert shook off the hands and straightened. "I most certainly can. What do you take me for?" He raised his chin, endeavoring to stare Stirling down, but his chin wouldn't stop. It went up and up. Robert's head tilted back. He'd never taken time to properly contemplate the ceiling of his club before. One always overlooked the details.

Four hands gripped him and stood him upright again when he started to topple backward. Stirling, still swaying, appeared greatly amused. He gestured and the hands began to half walk, half carry Robert.

The faces of other gentlemen at the club moved in a slow spiral around him as they crossed the room. Most were turned his way. Expressions ranged from sympathetic to disgusted. Robert would have taken careful note of who owned the latter, but the names of his peers were strangely absent from his brain. Maybe they were all named Geoffrey. The idea inclined him to laugh, but he didn't want to amuse Stirling any further.

The hands didn't toss him from the club as he half-expected, but instead took him up the steps and into one of the private rooms, furnished with a bed, desk, chairs and table. Inside stood a large, full washtub, as well. He had just enough sense to wonder why no steam rose from the tub before he was picked up and plunked, fully clothed, into the chilly water.

In shock, he slid under the surface. He came up gasping for air. Rapid blinking brought Stirling into view beside the tub. Robert unleashed a stream of invectives. Stirling gestured. A large hand settled on Robert's head and pushed him back under, then let him up immediately.

"Feeling better yet?" Stirling asked as Robert's head cleared the surface once more.

"You bloody, rat-faced, son-of-a—" A gesture from Stirling. Robert went down into the water again. He flailed at the hand, but it didn't remain on his head long enough to strike. He pushed himself to the surface, spitting water. "Do you mean to kill me?"

Stirling looked down at him, arms crossed, expression contemplative. "I thought death was your goal."

"You bloody well know it's not, you madman. This water is damned cold."

"Here in Scotland, we call it refreshing."

"Well I'm a bloody Englishman and I don't appreciate being dunked in a trough." Robert pushed a hand over his face, skimming away water. "What are you playing at, Stirling?"

"Playing?" Stirling shook his head. "No. I've a favor to ask, actually."

"A favor?" Robert gaped. He stood. Water streamed from his hair, coat, flattened cravat, everywhere. "This is you asking for a favor?"

"I need you clear-headed enough to comprehend my words." Stirling's tone was reasonable, but amusement lurked in his features.

Robert muttered a few choice curses as he stepped over the edge of the tub. Water sloshed across the floor. One of the footmen immediately began to wipe it up. The other offered Robert a towel, his expression neutral.

Robert took the proffered cloth and mopped at his face. "Look what you've done to my jacket. My vest." He let out another curse. "My boots, man. Look what you've done to my boots."

"Put them by the fire. John will take your clothes and see them made right."

Robert turned to take in the cheery blaze. Now that his vision was clearer, he also noticed a set of clothes laid out, as well as a nightshirt and robe. His clothes. His nightshirt and robe.

He cast Stirling an incredulous look. "You've been to my residence?"

"Yes. Your staff are rather worried about you. They haven't seen you in three days."

Robert shook his head, bemused. He crossed to the fire, then began stripping his lean frame. Stirling ordered the tub removed and the floor mopped. Robert shucked his sodden attire.

After toweling dry, he took up his robe. His original intention had been to dress, but weariness had settled. What was the point in dressing, after all? Once he heard Stirling out and sent him on his way, Robert could return to drinking just as easily in a private room in his robe as he could in the public room, dressed.

He belted his robe closed, plopped into an armchair and propped his feet on the nearby stool. He watched with little interest as servants gathered his wet garments, sopped up the last of the water and disappeared. The chair was near the fire, the warmth lulling. His eyes closed.

"Now, about that favor."

Robert forced his lids open to find Stirling seated on the other side of the fireplace. "The answer is no," Robert muttered.

"All I require is for you to attend three balls."

"Balls? With dancing?" Robert scowled. "With ladies?"

"That is generally the way of balls." Stirling rested his elbows on the arms of the chair and steepled his fingers before him.

"Can't. I've sworn off women. For good. No more." Robert shook his head, then regretted the movement as the room bounced. "I will not be jilted a third time, and certainly not again in Scotland. I'm leaving."

"Oh?" Stirling raised an eyebrow. "Headed back to London, are you?"

Robert looked away from those perceptive eyes. He could never go back to London. Every inch of the city reminded him of Cinthia. "Maybe the Continent. Perhaps even France."

"France? Do you intend to get yourself shot?"

Robert shrugged. "At least in France, when a man is jilted, he can drown his sorrow in cognac."

Stirling watched him over his steepled fingers.

Robert resisted an urge to squirm under that gaze. "Or I could hang about Edinburgh for a time. I've nothing against Scotland, just women."

With a sigh, Stirling brought his hands to the chair arms. "Miss Thomas did the right thing, breaking it off with you."

Robert went rigid. "What did you say?"

"Kitty Thomas did the right thing when she broke your engagement."

Anger coiled inside Robert.

"Anyone can see you're still in love with Cinthia."

Robert's anger disappeared like summer rain. Cinthia. The real reason he'd come to Scotland. For two years, they'd been engaged. In London, they were the toast of the *Ton*. Every dance, the theater, the park. Always together. Blissfully happy as they waited for her father to return from his government appointment in India so they could wed.

Then Lord Ailbeart had come along, with Scottish title. He enticed her with his lineage. Whispering that she was meant to be a member of the peerage, Lady Cinthia, Viscountess Dunreid. Not simply Missus Banbrook.

Fool that he was, Robert hadn't been worried. He'd believed in her. Believed in their love. Not until the morning he'd called round and learned she'd left for Scotland did he have any idea Viscount Dunreid had succeeded in his conquest.

He passed a hand over his eyes, weary. "What are you after,

Stirling? I've heard rumors of your new game, matchmaking." He eyed the other man. "I'm not looking for another woman to propose to. Twice was enough."

Stirling leaned back in his chair, his expression too innocent to be so. "The last thing I want to do is get some poor girl's hopes up with an introduction to you. Until you get over Viscountess Dunreid, you aren't fit for any woman." He shook his head. "No, I simply need you to help a certain young Miss stave off an aggressive gentleman long enough to find herself a good husband."

Robert frowned. "Stave off? She doesn't want to marry this gentleman? At least she's smart enough to realize as much."

"Aye, she seems an intelligent sort, but I believe the key issue is the offer of the gentleman in question. He wants her, but he has no intention of making her his wife."

So, a cad up to no good and apt to tarnish a young lady's reputation. "I see. She's in need of protection, then, not one of your quick weddings." He scrutinized Stirling. "Why don't you do help the girl?"

"I could, I suppose, but I wouldn't want to deprive you of the honor, or the amusement. Anyone can see you're in need of a bit of distraction."

Robert supposed there was some truth in that. Still, "Escorting some young Miss to dances doesn't sound particularly amusing." It sounded painful.

A sly grin formed on Stirling's face. "Oh, I daresay escorting this young Miss is just what you need. That, and a bit of revenge." He leaned forward in his chair. "You see, Banbrook, Dunreid wants the young lady for his mistress. You, my friend, are going to save her."

Other Marriage Maker Collections

Rules of Refinement Collection
One Good Gentleman
Shameless
Redemption of a Marquess
A Marriage of Necessity

The Marriage Maker Goes Undercover Collection
A Scoundrel in the Making
Her Wicked Highland Spy
My Lady of Danger
The Marriage Obligation

Daughters of Scandal Collection
The Lady in Pearls
A Lady's Book of Love
A Most Unusual Scandal
Brazen

The Original Marriage Maker Saga
Worth of a Lady
The Marriage Wager
A Lady by Chance
How to Catch an Heiress

www.scarsdalepublishing.com